Rabbit Moon

A Book of Holidays and Celebrations

by Patricia Hubbell

Illustrations by Wendy Watson

MARSHALL CAVENDISH • NEW YORK

Text copyright 2002 by Patricia Hubbell
Illustrations copyright 2002 by Wendy Watson
All rights reserved.
Marshall Cavendish, 99 White Plains Road, Tarrytown, NY 10591

Library of Congress Cataloging-in-Publication Data
Hubbell, Patricia.
Rabbit moon / Patricia Hubbell ; illustrated by Wendy Watson.
p.   cm.
Summary: Rabbits celebrate the passage of the year from month to month.
ISBN 0-7614-5103-X
[1. Months—Fiction. 2. Rabbits—Fiction. 3. Stories in rhyme.] I. Watson,
Wendy, ill. II. Title.
PZ8.3.H848 Rab 2002   [E]—dc21   2001042497

The text of this book is set in 14 point Cheltenham Book
The illustrations are rendered in acrylics and India ink.
Printed in Hong Kong
First edition

6 5 4 3 2 1

In Memory of my Mother and Father
Helen Eugenie Osborn Hubbell
Franklin H. Hubbell
Great Holiday Feast-makers!

—P. H.

January

Ringing bells, the Rabbits play,
Celebrating New Year's Day.

A brand-new year has just begun—
Twelve big months of Rabbit fun,
Filled with lovely things to do,
Holidays, and parties, too.

Now, Rabbits stand beneath the Moon
And each one sings this New Year's tune:

"Oh, Big-Rabbit-in-the-Moon,
Do you hop in flakes of white
Softly, softly, through the night?
Do you see our Earth-light shine?
Are your dreams the same as mine?

Now our New Year has begun—
Shine, O Moon, on Rabbit fun,
And on our Rabbit holidays
Turn your kindly silver gaze."

February

Rabbits hopping in the snow
Make a Rabbit Snowman grow.

His carrot ears and radish eyes
Watch and listen in surprise
As Rabbits pat out snow designs
And make him snowy Valentines.

On special nights, 'neath snow-bent cedars,
Rabbits praise old Rabbit leaders.
With speeches, songs, and one-act plays,
They honor them, these special days.

Rabbit Moon, from her high station,
Smiles to see the celebration.

March

March brings days of wind and chill
When Rabbits race on every hill.

Look! Look!
In the sky!
Rabbit kites
Go sailing by!

Now, Rabbits march in grand parades
While pipers pipe, in green berets.
Then, working in the lively breeze,
They dig their gardens, plant their peas.

March Moon shines down, as home they go,
Carting shovel, rake, and hoe.

April

Umbrellas bloom like pretty flowers
As Rabbits romp in April showers.

On April First, they joke and jest
As each one tries to fool the rest.

Showers pass. The Moon looks down—
And laughs to see the Rabbits clown.

May

Now, Rabbits pick fair flowers of May,
Nosegays sweet for Mother's Day.

Before the dawn, they rise to make
A special breakfast, with a cake,
To bring to Mama, warm and snug,
With many a loving kiss and hug.

The morning Moon, quiet and still,
Peeps above the window sill.

June

June brings Rabbit wedding days
When on their loved one, Rabbits gaze.

Paw in paw, two by two,
In ivy bowers, they say, "*I do.*"

The guests all feast on fresh young grass
And make a carrot arch, where pass
The wedded couples in their bliss,
Pausing many a time to kiss.

The dear Moon watches from above,
Shining on this night of love.

July

The night is dark. The Moon hangs low.
Now comes the Rabbit fireworks show.

Rabbits gasp and shout and sigh
At clover blossoms in the sky,
As on their quilts beneath the stars
They snack on green-bean candy bars.

Then home they traipse, to dream, to dream,
Of all the glorious sights they've seen.

August

Cabbage! Carrots! Lettuce! Cake!
Rabbits picnic at the lake.

Rabbits splash and jump and leap.
Grandpa Rabbit goes to sleep.

Baby Rabbits learn to swim.
Rabbit beanbag games begin.

Rabbits stay far into night
To see twin Moons—O lovely sight!

September

Off to school the Rabbits go.
Twenty Rabbits in a row.

With their friends, they read and write—
First time out of Mama's sight.

Playing games of every sort
They learn to share, and be good sports.

When school is done, they hoist their packs
And hurry home, to crunchy snacks.

When, at last, to bed they go,
They're bathed in old Moon's kindly glow.

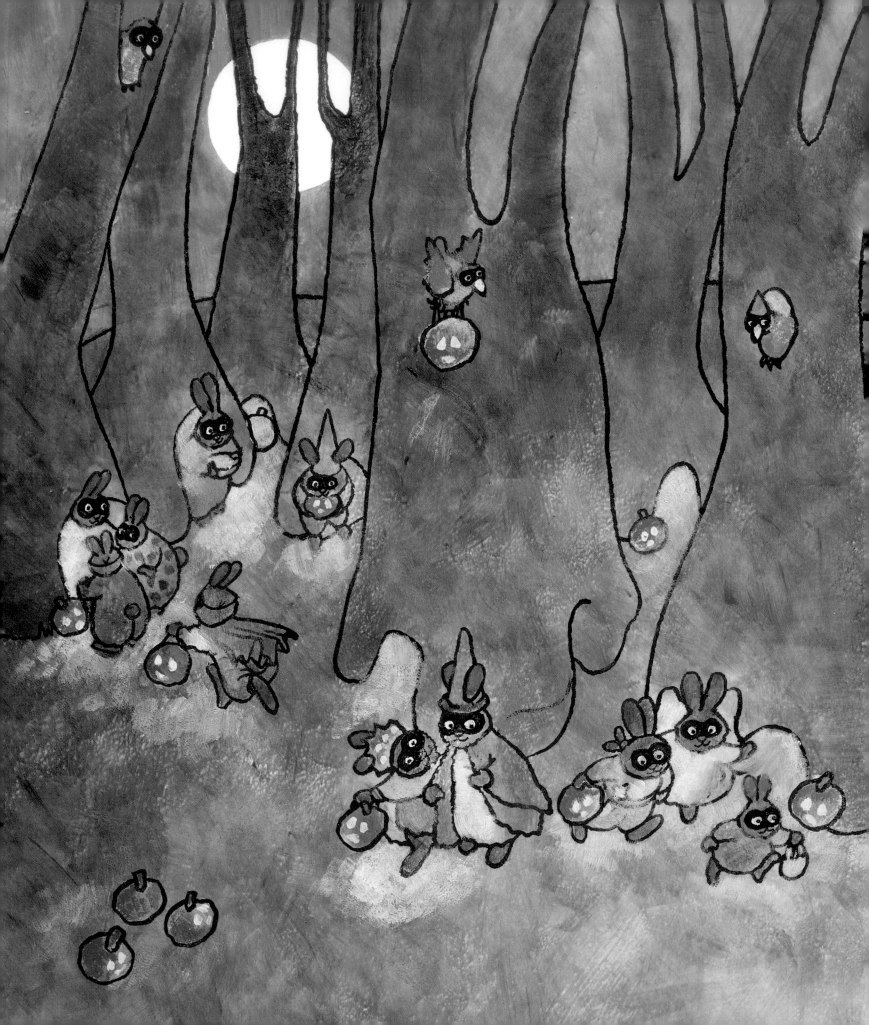

October

What a spooky, scary scene!
Rabbits dressed for Halloween!

On burrow doors they pound and beat
Demanding Rabbit trick-or-treat.

Then, by Moon and lantern light
They scuttle home, this eerie night.

They bob for apples, count their sweets
And brag about their frightful feats.

November

In the brisk November weather
Rabbit families join together.

To tables laden down with treats
They hop, skip, jump—and take their seats.

Before the luscious feast begins
They give their thanks for food and friends.

Beneath the Moon, each goes his way,
Grateful for this holiday.

December

At Rabbit windows, candles glow,
Casting light out on the snow.

Rabbit children whisper, scurry.
Rabbit mothers hurry, hurry.

Delicious smells fill the air.
Bustle, bustle, everywhere.

Gifts and joy and songs of praise
Fill this month of holidays.

As Rabbits watch, Moon-silver flows—
And Rabbit year comes to a close.

January, Again

Another Rabbit year is done.
A brand-new year has just begun.
Once more, beneath the Rabbit Moon,
Each Rabbit sings this New Year's tune:

"Oh, Big-Rabbit-in-the-Moon,
Thank you for your beams so bright
Shining through each Rabbit night.
Did you see our Earth-light shine?
Were your dreams the same as mine?

Old year's gone
And new's begun—
Shine, dear Moon,
On Rabbit fun.

And please, Moon, turn
Your kindly gaze
On our Rabbit holidays."

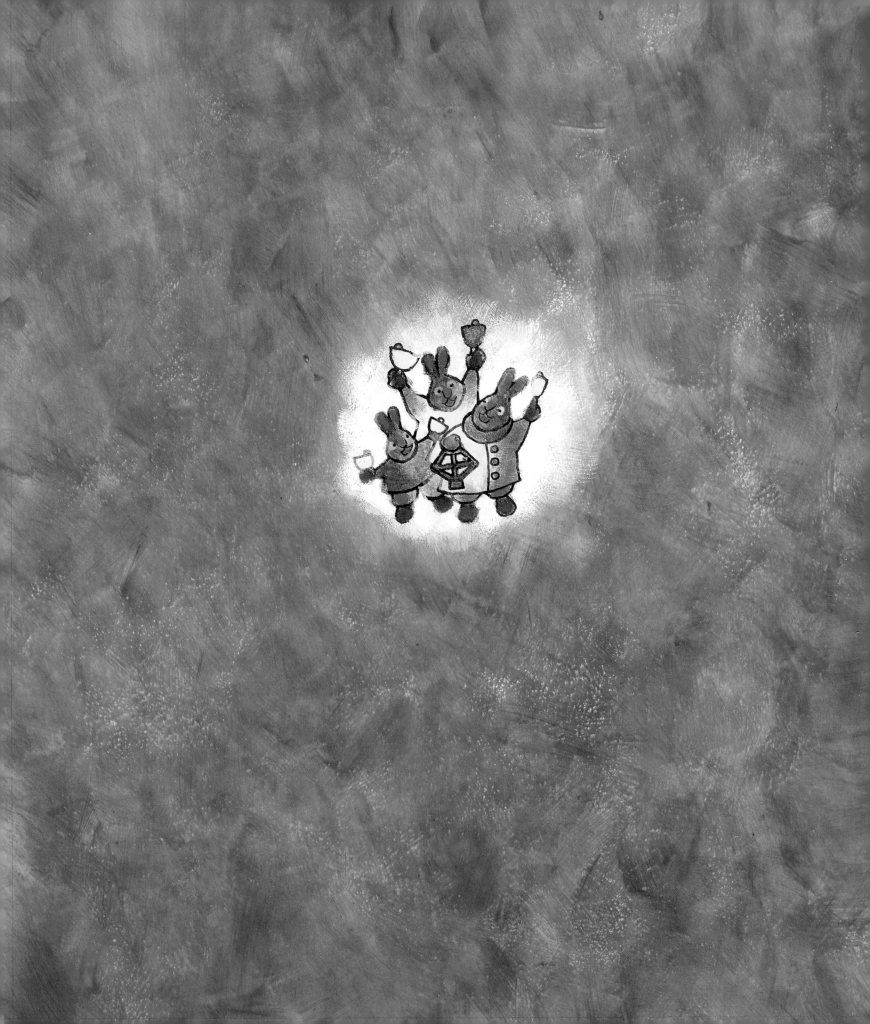